Izzie's Flora Day

by

Jude Carroll
with illustrations by
Lone Warberg

First published in 2007
by Helys Ventures
53 Wendron Street
Helston
TR13 8PT
01326 573781

ISBN 978-0-9555352-0-8
British Library Cataloguing -in-Publication data
A catalogue record for this book is available from the
British Library

Production by Liz Morrell
Printed by R. Booth Ltd, Mabe, Penryn, Cornwall, TR10 9HH

Acknowledgements

I am indebted to Patrick Carroll, Angie Munro,
Sue Pritchard, Val Boyd-Wallis, Cags Gilbert and all at
Constantine Primary School for encouragement; to
Zia Trevena for local wisdom; to Liz Morrell for help
and patience; to Mel Conoley and Nigel McKie for
their open doors and to Roger Clotworthy for the
spark of an idea.

This book is dedicated to all those who love Helston
on Flora Day and all the other days.

JANUARY

"Only one hundred and twenty seven days till Flora Day," announced Uncle Roger on the first day of January. Izzie smiled. She remembered him saying the same thing last year and the year before. For Uncle Roger, Helston Flora Day was the most important day of the year. It was more important than Christmas or his birthday. He was Helston born, Helston bred and one day would be Helston buried. Izzie's dad re-arranged the logs on the fire to make them burn more brightly. Uncle Roger sat back in

the armchair. The quiff of hair on top of his head moved about in lively imitation of his voice as he talked of Flora Days past and to come. Izzie listened to the tales familiar from re-telling and in her imagination the lights on the Christmas tree gradually transformed into dancers, dressed in purple and red, silver and gold. The glass angels strung between the branches became the town band winding up the hill and the glittering stars turned into a swathe of bluebells threading through the green foliage. When she woke, dad and Uncle Roger had gone for a pint of Spingo and Izzie's mum was busy in the kitchen preparing dinner. It was dark outside and there was frost in the air. Flora Day was a long time away.

FEBRUARY

Throughout February it rained nearly every day. When Izzie stepped outside her black front door, she couldn't see the hill beyond the town which normally marked the end of her field of vision; it was hidden in mist and drizzle. There were too many indoor playtimes at school and life was dull. One day, Izzie's dad told them he had to go away. He was being sent overseas to a country where a war was going on. He told them not to worry but Izzie watched the news sometimes and knew this place was dangerous. Izzie's mum became tense and very busy. Early on St Valentine's Day a car arrived for dad and they waved him goodbye in the half-dark of the dawn. Mum cried but Izzie suppressed her tears. That day at school, everyone was specially kind but the next day, someone knocked her over at playtime and barely said 'sorry'. She fell out with her best friend over whose turn it was to wash the paintbrushes and went home feeling miserable. A van speeding up her street covered her with muddy spray. Her mum tried to cheer her up but she slumped

FEBRUARY

moodily in front of the television till Uncle Roger popped in for a cup of tea and told her a joke. It helped.

MARCH

The March winds blew in from the Atlantic. The sea lashed the harbour walls in Porthleven and the little boats rocked at their moorings. One night the lifeboat was launched and rescue helicopters whirred overhead. Four people were saved and one was drowned. Izzie missed her dad. He was a long way away and didn't get in touch very often.

"He's busy," said mum, "and it's not always possible to send a message. He knows we're thinking of him and he thinks about us too. He'll be back soon." But mum didn't know when. She got annoyed if Izzie asked too many questions. Izzie drew dad pictures and wrote him notes. She told him about things she had done at school and about the new café where they sometimes

I hope you're back for Flora Day. Uncle Roger will be polishing his cornet soon and mum's friend Anna will be dancing in the early morning dance. She's making herself a dress from some dark red silk her grandmother brought back from India in 1936! Mum's going to be a hedge lady in the Hal-an-Tow so she just needs to make a costume out of an old curtain and cover it with leaves

went for lunch. She wrote 'I hope you're back for Flora Day. Uncle Roger will be polishing his cornet soon and mum's friend Anna will be dancing in the early morning dance. She's making herself a dress from some dark red silk her grandmother brought back from India in 1936! Mum's going to be a hedge lady in the Hal-an-Tow so she just needs to make a costume out of an old curtain and cover it with leaves.'

APRIL

One day Uncle Roger passed Izzie in the street as she was walking to school. He bent down to whisper in her ear.

"Just thought you'd like to know your skirt is caught up at the back and your knickers are showing," he murmured. For a split second Izzie panicked and put her hand behind her. Then she remembered what day it was.

"I'm no April Fool Uncle Rog, even if you are," she called, running to catch up with her friends. She turned to wave to him and he took off his jaunty cap to make her an elaborate bow. His eyes twinkled in the spring sunshine.

"Only thirty seven days to go!" he called.

An air of business and bustle pervaded the town during April. The days were warming and getting longer though there was still plenty of wind and rain driving over the hill and straight up Izzie's street. Everywhere, men in overalls climbed up and down ladders, painting, repairing and cleaning away the winter debris. There were advertisements in the pubs for extra staff. The local newspapers featured the honoured couples who would lead the midday dance and at school all the children who were old enough began to practise the Furry Dance, just as previous generations had. The children in Izzie's class chose partners and Izzie paired up with Jowan, the boy she had danced with last year. He wouldn't tread on her feet on purpose. Mrs Bassett put on the music and they stepped around the hall.

"Bums in, chests out and ......out together out, in together in, one two three hop – NO, not like a demented water buffalo, Sam Walker; with *dignity* please." After repeated sessions of this, most children had got the hang of what to do. Mrs Bassett didn't miss any chance to squeeze in a few minutes practice – even when it was a non-uniform day they danced in from the

playground, hand in hand. Izzie remembered from last year the sequence, it was just a question of brushing up.

On Tuesday evenings, mum nipped down to the Community Centre to rehearse the Hal-an-Tow. She went around the house singing the words to the song. She didn't sing in tune but told Izzie it was volume which mattered. Robin Hood, Spanish pirates,

St Michael, St George and the Dragon and someone called Mary Moses were all mixed up but the main idea was that good triumphed over evil in the end. Izzie felt quite proud of the fact that people from all over the world would come to celebrate Helston's big day and that a special law permitted the residents to pick wild flowers for the occasion. The April clouds scudded across the hills at the edge of the town, the apple blossom burst out on the old tree at the top of the garden and birds flew back and forth to their nests. Izzie spoke to her dad on the phone but his voice sounded remote and somehow different. He didn't talk to her about the fighting. She didn't tell him how much she missed him.

One day, mum brought home a crisp white dress with pearl buttons on the bodice and beads on the sleeves.

"Ugh," said Izzie, "I'm not wearing that. It's too ..... pretty. I want a plain dress, mum."

"But Anna has made it specially for you."

"I don't care. It's disgusting. I'd rather wear the same one as last year."

"But you can't. You've grown too tall," replied mum desperately. They argued. Mum tried every persuasive suggestion she could think of but Izzie was adamant. She would not be seen dead in that dress. Mum said she was ungrateful. Izzie said mum was mean to make her wear a dress she hated. She was very, very rude to her mum and was grounded. She stamped upstairs, slammed her door and threw herself on her bed to think about all the nasty things she would do to her mum if she had the chance. Dad would understand, but dad wasn't here. This time, Izzie didn't fight her tears. She sobbed her anger and sadness till her pillow was wet and a troubled sleep came over her.

The row about the dress festered for days, spoiling preparations for the big day. Izzie was stubborn and mum didn't like to ask Anna to change the dress. They communicated in curt questions and answers about essential matters such as food and homework. Izzie made faces at her mum behind her back. It was Uncle Roger who made the peace. He came for a cup of tea and a slice of chocolate cake, chatted about the band's preparations and how he was helping with the clean-up party to make sure the streets and waysides were spick and span. When he detected the frostiness between what he called his two favourite girls, he took away the dress, winked at Izzie and said, "Leave it it to me."

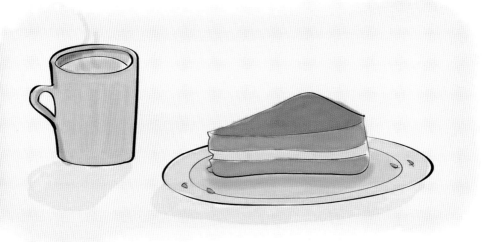

MAY

On the first day of May, Izzie woke at seven o'clock to the sound of the Furry Dance. She peeped through her bedroom curtains to watch the band striding below, leading a few dancing couples. No one was dressed up and it was a dull, damp beginning to the best month of the year but the familiar light-hearted tune lifted her spirits. She waved to Uncle Roger and he raised his cornet in salute, blowing a few notes specially for her as he passed by. On his back was pinned a large notice *'Only 7 days till Flora Day.'* Anna glanced up too as she and her partner turned arm-in-arm, using this early morning rehearsal as a last chance to perfect their dance steps. When she reached Izzie's door, in one swift movement she delved into her rucksack and took out a white dress which she hung on the big brass knocker, banging it once as she continued to dance. Izzie ran barefoot downstairs to unhook the dress. It was quite plain without pearl buttons or fancy beads and it fitted perfectly.

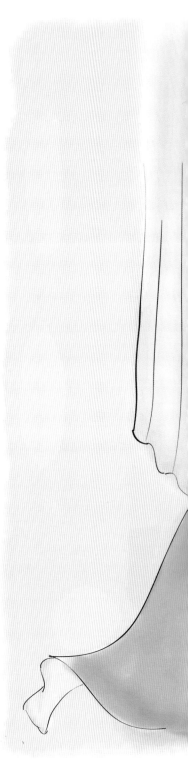

13

On the sixth day of May, Mum and Anna took baskets and scissors to a quiet place on the edge of town, where prickly yellow gorse crowned the top of a stone hedge. At its base bluebells and campion poked through the long grass. A stream ran on the other side of the lane and it was peaceful to gather arms full of wild flowers to the sounds of trickling water, pigeons and a mumbling bumble bee, the light scent of spring filling their heads. The long-stemmed bluebells were laid row on row, the white ends of their stalks sticky from their juices. Mum gathered the gorse in a thick plastic garden bag. Even wearing gloves, she scratched herself a few times. But she didn't seem to mind.

Getting a few grazes and pulling out thorns from fingers was all part of the preparation.

They made their way along the lane and into a small copse which was a haze of blue, filling their baskets as they went but being careful not to uproot any plants or pick a large number from one spot. However many they picked, there still seemed to be thousands left but at last, Izzie's mum decided they had enough so they returned home, feeling content. It then took some time to place the bluebells in all the available containers filled with water. The back yard was a mass of blue. Early tomorrow morning, mum would walk down the hill to the

Guildhall to collect some laurel, left for townsfolk to help themselves. When Izzie came home from school on Flora Eve, they would decorate the windows and the door. Izzie loved doing this. She fell asleep thinking about how the house would look, this time tomorrow.

FLORA EVE

The seventh day of May was a normal school day but with lots of notices about arrangements for the dance; where to assemble, what to do, what not to do, how to behave and so on and so on – all of which the children knew already but the teachers had to tell them again. The day dragged but at last the bell rang and the children piled out after final orders from Mrs Bassett about not being late tomorrow, or else. Izzie rushed home. Mum was already up the stepladder, fixing the last piece of trellis above the door. The brass eagle knocker and the number 53 were polished and shiny. Uncle Roger arrived to help but needed a cup of tea first, so they all went into the back yard. Izzie sat on

the bench, dividing the bluebells into even sized bunches. "Ten in a bunch is right, I think," she murmured to herself. The back yard was sheltered from the breeze and quite warm. The cat stretched lazily on the flagstones and the adults seemed in no hurry, making gentle conversation about ordinary things. In the background, the radio was on, with news of a helicopter crash. Anxiety suddenly punctured  Izzie's contentment. What was her dad doing right now? Was he sitting in an office? Was he outside in the fierce desert heat? Was he fighting someone?

"Let's get started," she said decisively, pulling the grown ups by the hands and leading them to the front of the house.

The two adults and the child were a good team. First they tied the laurel to the trellis with green string so it wouldn't show. Carefully Uncle Roger attached the gorse, muttering under his breath whenever a prickle caught him. Then they hung the bluebells. Izzie insisted they were evenly spaced and the same number at each window 'to make it fair'. They went back and forth to collect more flowers and foliage. Gradually, the buckets in the back yard emptied and only a few stems of wild leeks were left. Uncle Roger laced these into the arrangement on the windowsills.

"Your dad loves doing this," mused mum to Izzie, snipping off a stray twig. "We must take a photo for him when we've finished the job."

Izzie counted the bunches of bluebells. There were sixty-six of them.

"We picked six hundred and sixty bluebells yesterday, mum," she said.

"That's odd," replied mum. "It's the same number as your dad's squadron."

They stood back to admire their work from the far side of the road. Mum put her head to one side critically, then

disappeared indoors. A minute or two later, she returned carrying a sprig of apple blossom. She placed this in the centre of the laurel above the door.

"There," she said, "where's the camera?"

After tea, they wandered around the streets, admiring other people's handiwork. All day long, everyone in the centre of town had been busy. The shops in the main streets were decorated and nearly every house on the dance route had been dressed. Even the empty shops had been looked after by somebody. Now it seemed as if most of the population was doing the same as they were, strolling in the evening sunshine, smiling and greeting each other. As they walked by The Blue Anchor, sounds of laughter rang out and Izzie caught a glimpse of Uncle Roger raising a glass to his lips. His arm paused as he saw her.

"Only one more day," he called through the open window.

By the Monument next to the bowling green the Morris dancers were in full swing. They were leaping about, waving handkerchiefs and banging their sticks together. The bells on their knees and ankles jingled as they stamped their feet. A large crowd took delight in their enthusiasm and laughed when they bumped into each other. The dance ended to great applause and then the bystanders were invited to join in. The squire called out the moves and two long lines of people of all ages wove in and out, coached by the Morris men and accompanied by the drum, the accordion, the fiddle and an odd-looking stick with bottle tops nailed in called a lagerphone. Out of breath and laughing, Izzie and her mum left the crowd to make their way home, turning back now and then to gaze at the red-barred clouds above the hill which promised a fine Flora Day.

Curled in her bed, Izzie mentally checked what she had to do. The day would begin early and would be busy from start to finish, a long party with thousands of guests. The water in the open kennals at the side of the road babbled, and the sound of bells – church bells, Morris bells and telephone bells jingled and jangled in her sleep.

THE EARLY MORNING DANCE

They were up at six o'clock. Mum put the last touches to her Hal-an-Tow costume, which she must have been making till late into the night. No wonder she looked tired and distracted. The green curtain material had become a loose garment onto which were attached branches of sycamore and hazel, interwoven with trails of ivy so that very little fabric could be seen. Her head dress lay on the hall table – a crown of woven willow formed the base for a riot of leaves of varying shades of green. Beside it was Izzie's simple circle of green wire threaded with poppies and buttercups. Her plain white dress hung in the wardrobe and her special charm bracelet was ready in her jewellery case.

At half past six the church bells started to ring just as mother and daughter were sitting down to scrambled eggs on toast. Uncle Roger popped in on his way to the Guildhall.

"Just time for a cuppa before we begin," he said. "Happy Flora Day." By this time they could see through their window the hordes making their way down to the centre of town. The

spectators all wanted to get a good view of the first dance. Uncle Roger swallowed his tea quickly, squashed his quiff beneath his hat, adjusted his tie, straightened his uniform and strode off down the hill to join the band.

At seven o'clock exactly, Izzie and her mum heard the strike of the Guildhall clock coincide with the thud of the drum at the start of the familiar tune. Then they waited expectantly, straining to hear the band as it grew faint towards the top of Meneage Street. Excitement built as the tune grew louder when the band came back down and turned to march up their hill. They stood out on the street to see the crowds moving towards them, flanking the procession of musicians and dancers. Soon they drew level. The band led the way. Pride and happiness radiated from Uncle Roger as he fingered the valves on his cornet. Keeping the beat on the big bass drum was old Billy, whose job this had been for the last forty Flora Days. Then came the mayor, his chain of office lying importantly on his chest, accompanied by his stewards. The dancers followed. The young women wore pretty summer dresses, baring their shoulders to the chilly morning air. The young men were smart in white shirts, ties and new trousers. They were concentrating hard on their steps at the beginning of the route, not as relaxed as they would be by the time they finished their tour of the town. Maybe a hundred couples danced past Izzie's house, in amongst them Anna looked stunning in her dark red dress threaded with gold. Then they were gone. The band, the dancers and the crowds had wound their way through the narrow streets to a different part of town. "Quick," said mum. "Help me to get into my hedge." It wasn't easy to get the costume over mum's head. In the end, they went into the back yard and Izzie stood on the bench to lower it onto her shoulders. Mum put the head dress on and hung a whistle round her neck. The main point of the Hal-an-Tow was to make a lot of noise, driving away the bad spirits. Izzie thought that the great crowd of women, men and children surging from place to place to repeat their performance sounded louder than rowdy football hooligans. Just before mum rushed off to get to the starting point in good time, Jowan and his mother arrived, as arranged. With a few last instructions about where mum would be to see Izzie dance and where they would meet afterwards, mum rushed off like a green whirlwind down the street. After all the bustle and activity, there was now quite a lot of time before the children's dance began. The assembly point was conveniently right outside Izzie's house. Jowan changed in the spare room and Izzie put on her plain white dress in her bedroom. She brushed her hair and placed the circle of flowers on top.

Jowan's mother made it secure for her, and fastened the clasp on her charm bracelet.

"How pretty," she remarked.

"It was a present from my dad. He gave it to me three years ago to wear just on Flora Day," Izzie told her. "Really, we're not supposed to wear jewellery but I keep it tucked under my glove so Mrs Bassett won't notice." She didn't add that this was a source of disagreement with mum, who thought school rules should be obeyed and that the bracelet should only be worn once the dance was over. Jowan came out of the spare room looking cleaner than usual. His white trousers were sharply creased and his shirt ironed. His mother fiddled with the lily of the valley pinned to his chest. She also combed down his hair where it fluffed at the back and Jowan twitched away in irritation.

"You've got to look smart Jowan," she told him. "You never know who's going to take a photo of you or where the television cameras will be pointing."

Jowan's mother made herself some coffee and Izzie poured some orange juice.

"Don't spill it on your clothes now," warned Jowan's mother.

"And don't drink so much you get caught short half way round the town," she added. Jowan grimaced at Izzie but kept quiet. He had learned by experience not to argue. Crowds were collecting outside the house again. After a quick word to Jowan's mother they slipped out of the door to join the throng, gathering to watch the Hal-an-Tow.

THE HAL-AN-TOW

They heard the racket – calling and whistling and banging – as it got louder and louder. A disorderly rabble of oddly dressed people approached. In the space where two roads met, the hedge women formed themselves into a circle while the dancing maidens, the merry men, the pirates, the saints and the dragon waited outside the ring. Into the middle stepped the town crier, dressed in eighteenth century clothes of red and green, complete with lace cravat and buckled shoes. He rang his big brass handbell, calling "Clew ewgh! Clew ewgh! Clew ewgh!" and the crowd grew quiet. Then, continuing in Cornish "....Dun ny warbarth – an Hal-an-Tow a dhalleth...." After this

MAY

introduction, he translated a brief welcoming speech into English. The performers burst rumbustiously into the Hal-an-Tow song and the hedge began to move. Izzie scanned the green-dressed women for her mother. Her eyes darted around the moving circle and back again. She was nudged and jostled by the crowd and elbowed back fiercely. She forced her way to the front. Perhaps her mother's face was disguised under the head dress? So Izzie looked at the feet. Her mother was wearing distinctive dark green boots with pink laces. There were plenty of green sandals, brown shoes, black shoes, cream boots and even a pair of yellow flip-flops, but no dark green boots with pink laces. Mum wasn't there! St George killed the dragon amidst great cheers and St Michael vanquished the devil; the hedge circle loosened and the performers moved on noisily towards their next spot. Izzie went indoors in a state of perplexity. Where could mum be? She had been rehearsing the dance and the song for weeks. Surely she couldn't have quit because of nerves? Was she ill? Izzie started to panic as she thought of mum being lifted into an ambulance. Jowan's mother reassured her.

"Perhaps she just wanted a rest. Maybe she was a bit out of breath. Don't you worry now. Put on your head dress. It's your turn to get ready for the dance." As Izzie raised her arm to put on the circle of flowers, she saw her charm bracelet was gone. She let out a long wail and rushed out into the street to look for it but it was nowhere. It must have slipped off in the scrum of the crowd. Her precious, precious silver bracelet was lost. Her first thought was that it was her own fault, serving her right for disobedience, but she quickly banished that idea and blamed Jowan's mother. She couldn't have done up the clasp properly. Her bracelet and her mother had both disappeared. And where was her dad?

28

THE CHILDREN'S DANCE

Izzie lined up with Jowan in a daze. She was hardly aware of the pressing crowds, the cameras, the hubbub and mayhem surrounding her. Mrs Bassett, dressed as if for a smart wedding, just as all the other teachers were, asked her if she felt all right. She nodded absent-mindedly. She performed like a robot, her feet following the familiar pattern of their own accord. Out together out, in together in … Sometimes Jowan spoke to her and she answered without thinking. The onlookers were delighted by the scene before them. They were enthralled by the hundreds of white clad children stepping the ancient dance, the girls from each school identified by the flowers in their hair – poppies and buttercups, daisies, cornflowers or forget-me-nots.

The dancers moved to the continuously repeated tune and the band's instruments flashed in the clear morning light but Izzie was churning inside. Those in the crowd who knew her thought her worried expression was caused by concentration and were not bothered when she did not respond to their calls and waves. The dancers moved up and down the streets and past the shops. With the bluebells and greenery and fluttering flags as a setting, the scene made perfect material for hundreds of cameras. The turmoil of one young girl's thoughts was masked by the general gaiety of the occasion.

At the top of Meneage Street, Izzie peered at the crowd. This was the place where her mother said she would watch the dance. She should be standing outside Wills's. Izzie craned her neck over her shoulder, desperately searching. Her mother wasn't there. Anna stood in her place, still looking excited and happy. She aimed her new camera, indicating that Izzie should smile. Izzie managed a feeble grin but her eyes were bleak. Anna mouthed,

"See you later," as Izzie danced on. Wild thoughts raced through Izzie's mind. Mum hardly ever broke a promise. Something awful must have happened to her and losing the bracelet was a sign. By the time the dance was over and the children had been dismissed by their teachers with the exhortation to enjoy the rest of the day, Izzie was almost in tears. Anna, now wearing a cool cream linen jacket and trousers, met her with the words,

"Well done princess. Now we have an appointment to keep."

"Will mum be there?" asked Izzie. Anna was evasive.

"Er ... something came up. You'll see her later."

"She missed the dance. Where *is* she?" Izzie's anxiety was beginning to turn to anger. How dare her mother behave like this? Something was going on and it wasn't fair that she was being kept in the dark.

THE MIDDAY DANCE

Izzie had often passed the handsome house on the corner below the church but had never been inside. Today, however, was different. Anna took her in by the side door and through to the courtyard. The sun was overhead and its heat was trapped by the pale stone walls. The noise of the celebrations outside could not be heard at all amongst the chatter of the guests. There were a lot of people here, dressed in pale summer clothes brightened by flashes of turquoise and yellow. The women, eyes hidden behind sunglasses, looked unfamiliar. These people whom Izzie didn't know stood or sat in groups, chatting politely to one another and nibbling olives or little tarts. Anna greeted several people by name, shook some hands, kissed a few cheeks. She introduced Izzie and people made pleasant remarks about the children's dancing. A waitress threaded her way through the people and the exotic potted plants, handing round glasses of wine from a tray. She gave Izzie a tall glass of squash with wedges of orange and lemon, with lots of crushed ice. Izzie slipped away while Anna talked to a distinguished-looking man with grey hair. She sipped her squash as she wandered about the courtyard, apparently the only child. Round a corner, she discovered a rectangular fish pond with a fountain at the far end. It wasn't so hot here. She crouched down to trail her fingers amongst the fronds of weed and watch the koi carp glide

languidly below. She puzzled about her mother. Was she coming to meet her here? Did she know these people? Or was there a cover up? Was Anna looking after her because something had happened? Or had mum got so fed up with her she had decided on the spur of the moment to go away? Izzie thought about the times when she had been horrible and cross and hadn't helped as much as she should have done. She really should not have been so stubborn about wanting a plain dress or wearing her bracelet. It was difficult, without dad being there but she should try harder. After a while, Izzie became aware that she wasn't alone. A pair of large shiny brown shoes were planted next to her and she looked up into the kind face of an elderly gentleman. He wore a panama hat and was carrying a newspaper. Izzie noticed that he had filled in the clues on the crossword in green ink.

"You look a little bit fed up young lady. Though also very charming with your white dress and flowers in your hair. Something on your mind?"

Then Izzie found herself crying and blurting out to this stranger that she missed her dad, her mum had disappeared and she had lost her very special bracelet. This was turning into the very

worst Flora Day ever. The nice gentleman took her by the hand, fished a clean handkerchief out of his pocket to dry her tears and led her towards the house just as a bell sounded. The company made their way through to the front of the house in an orderly fashion, their steps echoing on the polished oak floor of the spacious hall. Anna took Izzie's other hand, which she squeezed excitedly. They walked down the front steps, watched by hundreds of people in the street. Izzie felt important. She

MAY

was on the inside of the iron gate, they were outside. Everyone was expectant. The families who lived in Helston and those who had returned for this day from as far away as Quebec and California and Queensland were waiting for a glimpse of the famed midday dance. The Rowes and the Williams, the Tresidders

and the Treloars, the Bassetts, the Penroses and the Polglases were meeting and greeting and hugging and waiting for the dance.

The double doors stood open. The columns of the portico on top of the steps were wound about with blue and green and yellow. All eyes were focused on that doorway. Time passed. The crowds continued to mill and people to chat, babies cried in the crush. In the front garden, the guests carried on sipping their drinks and adjusting their hats to keep out the sun. Then, the sound of the band could just be heard somewhere behind the house. There was movement in the hall. The dignitaries emerged, then the musicians, smart in royal blue jackets trimmed with gold, instruments glinting in the sunlight. With a flourish, the first midday dancers stood in splendour for a moment at the top of the steps. She was dressed in a froth of fuchsia pink with a wide-brimmed feathery hat. He was tall and handsome in his morning suit, complete with grey top hat and lily of the valley in his buttonhole. The crowds murmured appreciatively. Down the steps came the couple, hands held up high, gloved fingers touching. Behind them came another couple, equally fine in their Flora Day regalia. Then another and another. Two by two they descended the steps, some of them with dignity, others faltering, perhaps confused by all the attention they attracted. Comments were made about each dress as it came into view. The styles varied from wide and flouncy to clinging and sensuous. Some hats were like huge saucers, others neat and closer fitting. The men's suits varied little and all had lily of the valley on the lapel. Their figures were different; some short and tubby, others tall and skinny and all body shapes and sizes in between. Everyone looked pleased to be taking part. The stream of couples was seemingly endless but the attention of the crowd didn't waver. All delighted in seeing the fine clothes paraded before them on a bright May day. What could be a better celebration of the season? Even Izzie put her troubles to the back of her mind. She still held hands with Anna and the nice old gentleman as the couples in the procession tripped down the steps and out through the iron gate. A plump middle-aged lady in a green gown, long green gloves and floppy hat tittered as she placed each foot carefully step by step in turn, making a remark to Anna that it wouldn't do to spoil her dignity by taking a tumble. Her equally plump partner held her hand tightly in a steadying grip.

"Careful now, Beryl, " he said sternly. "You're not dressed for giggling." Behind this couple, Izzie saw a tall woman emerge from the dark of the house, wearing strappy red high-heeled sandals, a short gold jacket and a dark red dress, threaded with gold. Surely this was Anna's dress? But Anna was here beside her. She looked again as the woman stepped down. Under the net of the red hat, her mother's eyes met hers and twinkled mischievously. Her partner, his hat placed saucily to the side of his head to show a mop of unruly hair, was grinning broadly straight at her. Izzie squealed with joy and could not stop herself rushing towards him. He paused on the bottom step, caught her in his arms and swung her once around. Izzie heard the audience clap and cheer loudly as if they had been expecting this to happen. Then mum and dad were whirled away by the crowd and the second section of the band descended the steps to more applause. Uncle Roger was still as bright and shiny as he had been in the early morning, enjoying his special day to the full.

Izzie pulled Anna through the gate, "Come on," she said, "We'll catch up with them at the next stop." Further along the street, the large garden of the house called Lismore was open to the

public for this day only. Izzie and Anna were caught up in the movement of the mass of people also making their way to the garden, through the gates, along the path and out onto the lawn, which sloped to a small lake. At the far side of the lake, under the trees which wore fresh spring leaves, dancing through the fringe of bluebells, a line of figures was mirrored in the water. As each pair completed the circuit of the lake, they peeled off to join the spectators, to have a rest and a glass of champagne before continuing on their way. At the very end, the rakish top hat and the red and gold dress came into view and at last Izzie was in her father's encircling arms. The three of them sat on the grass and Izzie was told the full story. Dad had phoned mum late last night to tell her he had a few days special leave and as they had been given an invitation to dance the midday dance before he went away, it seemed such a shame not to do it after all. So Anna had been enlisted as last minute provider of clothes and dancing instructions.

"And we wanted to make a lovely surprise for you," finished mum.

THE EVENING DANCE

Later that day, they followed the last dance home. As the strains of the Flora Day tune faded into the distance for the last time, mum, dad and Izzie danced, slightly awkwardly as a threesome, up the hill to their house. The flowers at the window were wilting now and some were lying squashed on the pavement but Izzie did not feel sad. It had turned out to be the best Flora Day ever. Mum turned the key in the lock and she and dad went in together. Izzie felt that good really had triumphed and summer had come at last when, caught in the foliage at the side of the door, she glimpsed the sparkle of her special silver bracelet. It hadn't been lost after all.

MAY

MAY

As Izzie was closing her window before going to bed, she took once last look at what was left of Flora Day. What she saw was Uncle Roger, twinkling brightly from the excitement of the day and maybe a pint or two of Spingo, wobbling up the hill, his cornet tucked under his arm. He wished her goodnight and then added, as an afterthought,

"Only three hundred and sixty five days till Flora Day."